THIS WALKER BOOK BELONGS TO:

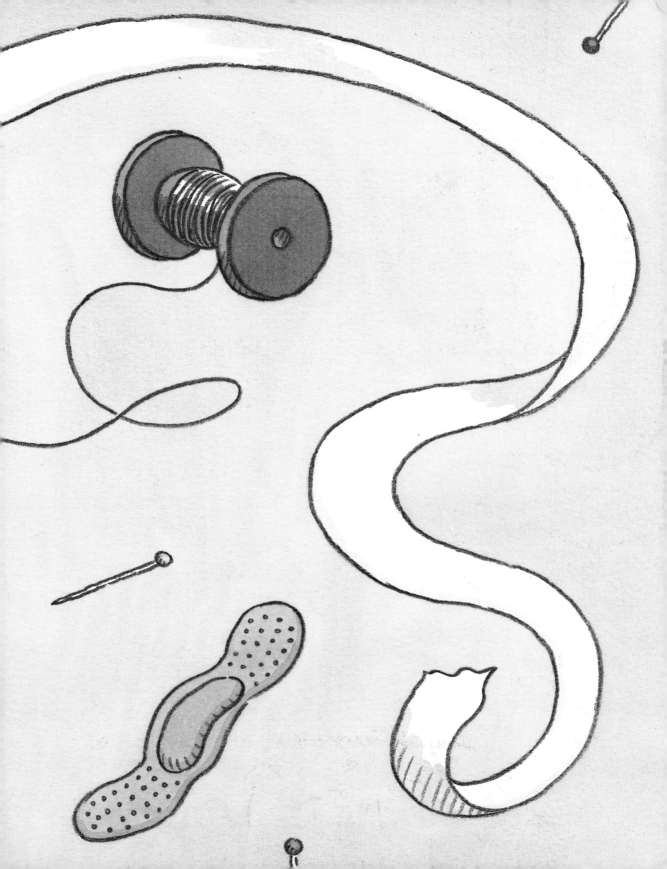

First published 1991
by Walker Books Ltd, 87 Vauxhall Walk
London SE11 5HJ

This edition published 1993

© 1991 Dom Mansell

Printed and bound in Hong Kong by
South China Printing Co. (1988) Ltd.

British Library Cataloguing in Publication Data
A catalogue record for this book is available
from the British Library.

ISBN 0-7445-3057-1

My Old Teddy

Dom Mansell

WALKER BOOKS
LONDON

My old Teddy's leg came off.

Poor old Teddy!

I took him to the Teddy doctor.

She made Teddy better.

My old Teddy's arm came off.

Poor old Teddy!

I took him to the Teddy doctor.

She made Teddy better.

My old Teddy's
ear came off.

Poor old Teddy!

I took him to the Teddy doctor.

She made Teddy better.

Then poor old Teddy's head came off.

The Teddy doctor
said Teddy's had
enough now...

Teddy has to rest.

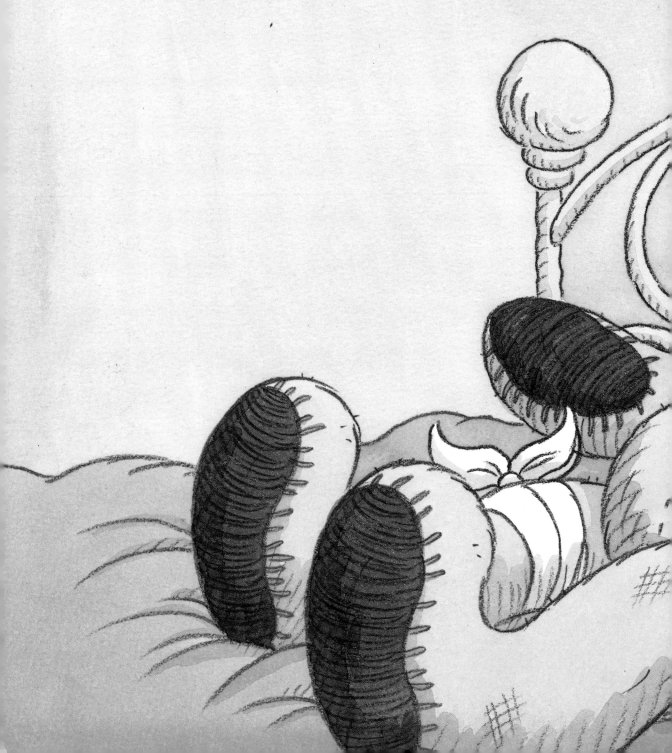

The Teddy doctor gave me...

my new Teddy.

I love new Teddy
very much,

but I love
poor old Teddy best.
Dear old,
poor
old
Teddy.

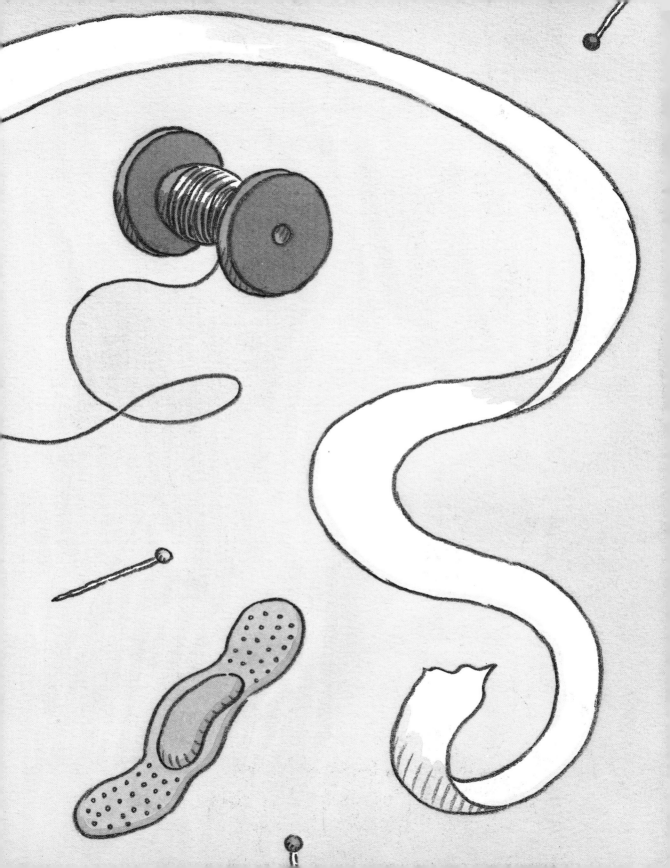

MORE WALKER PAPERBACKS
For You to Enjoy

Also illustrated by Dom Mansell

JUDY THE BAD FAIRY
by Martin Waddell

"A crazy romp about a lazy fairy… The scatty drawings
brilliantly evoke the mayhem which Judy provokes."
John Lawrence, The Times Educational Supplement

0-7445-1764-8   £2.99

MY GREAT GRANDPA
by Martin Waddell

A book about the very special relationship between the young and the very old.

"Charming story… Expansive, detailed pictures."
School Library Journal

0-7445-2011-8   £3.99

THE SELFISH GIANT
by Oscar Wilde

"A classic and poignant tale… Dom Mansell's delightful illustrations
are both colourful and full of amusing detail."
BBC Radio

0-7445-1412-6   £3.99